written by JESSICA SCHRODY   illustrated by LEAH GIBBONS

MOMMY, CAN YOU RAP ME A BEDTIME STORY?

Copyright © 2021
She Really Had A Baby, LLC.
All Rights Reserved. No part of this book May Be reproduced and or used in any manner without the prior written permission of the copyright owner.

Jessica Schrody
Jessicarose@shereallyhadababy.com
Shereallyhadbaby.com

To my daughter Nylah -
"You have to move out when you're eighteen."

There lived a family of two, a beautiful girl, and a wonderful mommy that would give her the world.

While the mommy would work, the girl learned and played, until the mommy came back at the end of the day.

Once dinner was finished, it was time for a bath - full of bubbles and laughter. Then they'd practice math.

As the little girl yawned, she climbed into bed in a hurry. She asked, "Mommy, can you rap me a bedtime story?"

Her mommy sighed deeply, as she turned off the lights. Then she picked up a book and picked up a mic.

"Check one two, one two!"
She said. "Coming to the stage -
I mean, coming to the bed."

"The coolest kid on earth,
I've ever seen. At dinner tonight,
she ate all of her greens."

The little girl giggled and cheered on her mother. Her eyes swelled with pride because she knew her mom loved her.

Her mom kept on rapping,
"I don't need a beat. You gon' fall asleep.
You got stinky feet."

The little girl's eyelids soon became as heavy as rocks. She felt warm and cozy in her pajamas and socks.

Her mother took notice that she fell asleep, but just to make sure, she stayed on the beat.

"My baby and I are the best of friends! I love her so much I even tuck her in."

She kissed her on her forehead and stroked her cheek. Then she went to the kitchen to make a cup of tea.

She read and got some work done. Then laid next to her child, where she closed both of her eyes and rested for a while.

Jessica Schrody, a Los Angeles native, is best known for breaking out of boxes, flipping scripts, and speaking the hand-to-God truth. In 2017, she created her wildly popular brand, She Really Had A Baby, where she began using her quick wit and humorous insights to change the negative stigma about being a baby mama.

Jessica Schrody
The Author

Over the course of four years, Schrody has built a community of ride-or-die followers across all social platforms and plans on continuing to write, rap and joke her way across the internet and into the hearts of mothers in all relationship statuses. Her newest children's book, **"Mommy, Can You Rap Me A Bedtime Story?"** is the perfect intersection of her talents as both a writer and an entertainer. To learn more about Schrody, visit:

https://www.shereallyhadababy.com/

CPSIA information can be obtained
at www.ICGtesting.com
Printed in the USA
BVHW020213210221
600682BV00002B/6